Firewatch

by Margo Sorenson

To Jim, Jane, and Jill, the world's best support crew.
To Geoff, who puts out fires, both on the printed page and
in the real world.

M. S.

Cover Illustration: Darren J. Evans
Inside Illustration: Michael A. Aspengren

Contents

1

Riley Arrives

"Judd! Judd!"

Judd looked past the corral fence to where his mom called to him from the Jeep.

"Hurry up! Your father's waiting for you. You've got a lot of fence to mend," she called.

"Okay!" he shouted. He waved at her. She waved back and drove away down the dirt road.

Dust billowed after the red Jeep. The hot, dry summer had already baked Wells Valley to a dusty brown. Even the creek just barely trickled through the valley.

Judd threw the saddle over his horse, Cab. "A lot of fence to mend," he grumbled aloud. He buckled the girth under Cab. "Summer's almost more work than school!" he said to her.

Judd patted her neck. "Yeah, Cab," he said. "You don't know how lucky you are to be a horse. No mending fences for you. And you don't have to put up with Riley Preston all summer, either." Judd frowned.

Riley's grandparents owned the next ranch over. But Riley was a city kid. That wasn't the problem, though. Other city kids visited relatives in the valley all the time. They were all fine. It was just Riley who wasn't.

When Riley's parents couldn't handle him, they'd send him to his grandparents. That was most of the last two summers. And Riley was due to arrive today. The rest of Judd's summer would be ruined for sure.

Judd wondered what it would be like to have your parents not want you around. He shook his head. Sure, he complained about some of his parents' rules and the chores he had to do. But he'd hate to get sent away. And by his own parents too.

Cab shifted her weight. She set a hoof down near Judd's boot.

"Whoa, girl," Judd said, quickly stepping out of the way. "Watch where you're stepping, will ya?" He grinned.

Judd headed over to the gate. He unlatched it and the gate swung open. Then he walked back across the corral.

Holding the reins in one hand, he grabbed the saddle with the other. He put one boot in a stirrup. Then he jumped up and swung his other leg over Cab.

"Okay, girl," he said. With one hand, he reached down and patted her neck.

"Come on, Tracker," he called to his dog. "Tracker?"

Tracker trotted up. He panted, his tail wagging.

Judd yelled toward the ranch house. "Hey, Teddy, can you shut the gate?"

Judd's little brother raced down the wooden steps and called, "Sure!"

Teddy grinned and shut the gate.

Judd sat up in the saddle. "Let's go mend fences," he said, squeezing Cab's sides with his knees.

Judd looked around him as he rode up the dirt road. The dry, hot summer had scorched the hills. The dry grass was yellow and brown. Dusty-looking live oak trees gave some shade to the hills.

The hills became mountains way behind his family's ranch house. Up there, live oaks gave way to dark green pines. Blue sky framed the tall peaks.

Judd reined in Cab. From where Judd sat, he could see the whole of Wells Valley. It spread out below his family's ranch. Other ranches dotted the valley. From way up here, the cattle looked like toys grazing in the dry grass.

The creek bed looked parched. Ranchers were trying to save water, but it was hard. Ranches needed a lot of water.

Because of the extra dry, hot weather they were having, most ranchers had cleared brush around their houses. It was the law. They had to do it.

Judd's thoughts drifted to what he'd rather be doing. He loved to spend time at the Wells Valley fire station. Andy and Pete were the two captains there. Judd enjoyed listening to their stories. And they liked having him around too.

Every spare minute he had, Judd rode over to the station to visit. Everyone would grin when he came. Tim and Cord would elbow him. Judd wanted to be a firefighter someday. "Can't wait to be a hotshot, eh?" they'd all tease.

Today Judd wished he could hear the latest news from Andy. Big forest fires were blazing in Northern California. They'd been burning for a week. Andy said this was one of the worst fire seasons ever. He couldn't remember when it had been this dry.

Judd kept walking Cab up the trail through the dry oak trees. Judd knew his dad was waiting at the creek.

Tracker trotted ahead. His tail waved like a flag.

"Hey!" Judd said as he grabbed his hat. Cab had drifted to the trail's edge, and a low branch had almost swished it off. He steered Cab back to the center.

He noticed how dry the leaves were. The brittle grass

brushed against Tracker when he left the trail to hunt for squirrels.

Judd's thoughts returned to firefighting and the Wells Valley fire station. Tim and Cord were seasonals there. During the year they went to college. In the summer, they fought fires. The county fire department hired guys just for the summer fire season. Some of them had other jobs in the winter.

In a few more years, he could be a seasonal, like Tim and Cord. Then he wouldn't have to spend his summer mending fences and putting up with Riley Preston.

Then when he was older, Judd looked forward to becoming a hotshot. The hotshots stayed together in crews of 20 guys. They fought fires right on the fire lines. Judd couldn't wait to be old enough.

"Judd! Hey, son, wake up!" His father's voice broke into Judd's thoughts.

Judd blinked. He saw his dad through the trees sitting on his big black horse, Flyer.

"You're late," Whit said. "Where've you been? Down bothering people at the fire station?"

Judd's heart sank. His dad knew Judd dreamed of fighting fires. But he wanted Judd to become a rancher—and run the Bar Vee someday.

Judd kicked Cab to a trot. "No, Dad," he said. "I wasn't." He wished he had, though. It'd sure be better than mending fences.

His brother Teddy liked all this ranch stuff. So he

could run the family ranch someday. But there was no way *Judd* would do it. He couldn't imagine being stuck on a ranch when he could be fighting fires.

Sure, it was dangerous work. Firefighters got injured. They even died. But they were heroes. They saved lives. They saved forests too.

"The fence posts and wire are stacked up yonder," Whit said. "I had Bart drive them up yesterday." Bart was their hired hand. He was laid up with a broken leg. He wouldn't be much help for a while.

Together Judd and his dad rode along the fence. They strung barbed wire and hammered in fence posts. The sun rose higher in the sky.

Judd wiped his forehead. They had been working for a long time, and he was ready for a break. He thought his dad would never stop.

Finally, Whit stopped and looked at Judd. He tipped his hat back on his head and grinned. "Ready for lunch?" Whit asked.

"Thought you'd never ask," Judd said. He mopped his neck with his bandanna.

"Come on, Tracker," Judd called. He and his dad mounted their horses and walked them slowly down the trail. Birds sang in the trees above their heads.

Tracker frisked around the horses. "Yes, Tracker," Judd said. "Back to the ranch."

Judd kept an eye on the brush next to the trail. He watched for movement. A snake or chipmunk might spook Cab.

Cab was a good horse. But she didn't like surprises—no horse does. She would rear up. Judd would fight to stay in the saddle. But all was quiet. A breeze fluttered the oak leaves.

VROOOM! VROOOM! The harsh whine of an engine cut through the stillness.

Cab whinnied and reared. She threw her head up. Her forefeet pawed the air.

"Whoa, girl!" Judd called. He shortened the reins. Cab settled down.

Judd's father reined in his horse.

VROOOM! VROOOM! There it was again. The sound echoed through the trees. It seemed to come from over the ridge. Judd held the reins tightly.

"What the heck is *that?*" Judd asked his dad.

Cab sidestepped. Judd leaned over and patted her neck. She whinnied softly.

Whit shook his head. "Sounds like a motorcycle, doesn't it?"

They began walking their horses again.

"What fool would ride a motorcycle up here?" his dad asked in disgust. "Scare the cattle? Raise more dust? Send sparks into the dry brush? Must be some city fool."

2
The Show-Off

Judd looked over at his dad.

"There's only one city fool I know of around here," Judd said. "Riley."

"The Preston kid?" his dad asked.

Just then, they reached the corral gate. "Ho!" Judd said to Cab.

Tracker jumped through the gate crossbars. He stood in the corral with his tail wagging. His tongue lolled from his mouth. He barked.

"Yeah, we're coming," Judd told him, grinning.

"I'll get it!" Teddy yelled from the barn.

In the distance, Judd heard the motorcycle sputtering. "There it is again," he said to his father.

Whit pressed his mouth into a thin line. "Bud and Minnie Preston'll have their work cut out for them, all right," he said.

Teddy hurried around the corner of the barn. He unlatched the gate.

"I'm almost done cleaning the tack room, Dad," he said. "It looks good."

"Good for you, Teddy," Whit replied, looking pleased.

Judd winced. How could Teddy always be so happy about ranch work?

Judd and his dad rode through the gate. Teddy closed it. "I'll see you inside for lunch," he called. His boots clattered up the steps.

Judd dismounted. He tied the reins to the fence.

"Now, what were you saying about the Preston kid? Why are you so sure he's on that motorcycle?" his dad asked. They began unsaddling their horses.

"Last time Riley was up here, he bragged about a motorcycle. Memorial Day weekend. Remember the big barbecue at the Legion Hall?" Judd asked.

Judd hung the saddle over the fence rail. Then he took the saddle pad off Cab and shook it.

"Oh yeah," his dad said. "I remember. That Riley sure is a mouthy kid, ain't he?" He began brushing down Flyer.

"Uh-huh," Judd agreed.

Judd slid the bit out of Cab's mouth. Then he reached up and took off the bridle.

"All he could talk about was his motorcycle," Judd continued. "His parents got it for him. Like he's not spoiled enough already." Judd made a face as he brushed down Cab. He gave Cab a slap on her rump. She trotted off.

Judd and his dad began walking across the yard to the house. "Yep," Whit said. "I feel sorry for Bud and Minnie. It must be tough on them having Riley around so much. They already raised one family.

"It's a tough situation all the way 'round," Whit continued. "I guess Riley's parents have their problems too. Especially the father."

Judd frowned. "Riley kept bragging about his hot dirt bike. He said he wanted to bring it up here to the valley," Judd said, following his dad into the mud room.

They cleaned their boots off. Judd began tugging on his boots.

"Andy heard Riley bragging," Judd said between tugs. "He told him to leave it in the city. That motorcycles weren't a good idea in the valley," Judd continued. "Especially during fire season."

"Captain Andy knows what he's talking about," Whit

agreed. "Ranchers have no love for motorcycles. They stampede cattle. They spook horses. And they raise a heck of a lot of dust. Which we have plenty of this summer in the valley." Whit propped his boots up under the bench.

"Don't forget about fire danger," Judd reminded him. He picked foxtails off his jeans. "That's probably the worst part."

Judd's mother put her head around the corner of the mud room. "Lunch is ready," she said smiling. Then she went back into the kitchen.

Judd and his dad followed her. They washed their hands at the sink.

"But motorcycles have spark arresters, right?" Judd's dad asked. He sat down and looked at the sandwiches. "Looks good, Arella," Whit said with a smile.

Judd took a chair at the table. He poured himself a glass of milk. A pile of sandwiches sat on the table.

"What are you two talking about?" Judd's mother asked. "What's all this about motorcycles and spark arresters?" She passed the plate of sandwiches.

"I know!" Teddy exclaimed. His eyes widened. "I heard it. The motorcycle, right?"

Judd's mom creased her forehead. "Say, I heard something too. I thought at first it was just a chain saw. It came from the Preston place. But then it raced off." She poured a glass of milk for Teddy. "It wouldn't be Riley, would it?"

"Uh-huh," Judd said. He swallowed a bite. "I sure think so." He frowned. "If it is, there'll be nothing but problems the rest of the summer. Riley's already an idiot. On a motorcycle, he'll be even worse."

"Now, Judd," Arella said. She frowned a little at him. "I feel sorry for the Prestons," she said. "Bud and Minnie are such nice people. How sad to have a grandson like Riley."

Judd's mother took a bite of her sandwich. Then she looked at Judd. "But you be nice to him. You hear?" she asked. "He's had it rough with his dad's drinking and all."

Judd almost choked on a bite of tuna. "Nice! *Nice?* To that jerk?" he sputtered. "No way!"

"Listen, son," Whit said. He lowered his eyebrows. "The Prestons are special friends. They've helped us out in some pretty tough times." He looked hard at Judd. "And besides, they're valley people.

"Take Riley along if you go somewhere. Give him a chance. He may have grown up some. Do it for Bud and Minnie," he finished.

Judd looked down at his sandwich. Be nice to Riley Preston? They had to be joking. Riley was an A-Number-One Idiot.

Riley by himself was bad enough. Riley on a motorcycle would be disaster. He'd think he was somebody great for sure.

None of the ranchers would be happy about Riley's motorcycle either. But for his grandparents' sake, they'd probably keep quiet.

Riley hated horses and ranch life. So the Prestons would probably let Riley ride his motorcycle, just to give him something to do. And to keep him out of their hair.

Judd took another bite of sandwich.

VROOOM! VROOOM! There it was again. And it was coming closer. Everyone looked up.

Soon a motorcycle sputtered outside in their yard. "Hey, Vandorf!" a voice yelled over the noise. "Hey! Come on out here!"

It was definitely Riley's voice. Judd sighed.

"Better go, son. Tell him to cut the engine," Whit frowned. "It'll spook the horses."

"Okay," Judd said. He got up.

In the mud room, he pulled on his boots. He walked through the door and stood on the porch.

Sure enough, Riley was circling the yard on a red motorcycle. He gunned the engine. Clouds of dust swirled up.

Tracker bounded down the steps. He barked furiously at Riley. Judd hid a smile. Track always could tell what someone was really like.

Riley stopped under a big oak tree. He grinned. "Cool, huh?" he asked. He squeezed the throttle again. VROOOM! VROOM! The engine raced.

"Yeah," Judd said half-heartedly. He winced.

Riley tossed the hair out of his eyes. "I told you I had one," he said proudly. "Want to ride it?"

Judd walked across the yard toward Riley. "Not now," he said. "Cut the engine, would you?"

Judd looked over at the horses in the corral. They stood at the far end. Cab's ears were flattened against her head. Whit's horse nervously pawed the ground. The horses in the barn were probably going nuts.

Riley looked disappointed. He cut the engine. "Yeah, okay. I forgot what a bunch of nature-lovers you all are up here." He rolled his eyes.

"Nature-lovers?" Judd repeated with disgust. "It's just common sense. You can't spook the horses." He folded his arms and stared at Riley.

Riley leaned back in the seat. "Horses this, cows that. What a bunch of hick ranchers," he said. "Except you, of course," he added quickly as Judd's face darkened.

"Yeah?" Judd asked, trying to control his anger. "Well, watch your mouth around the valley. You may end up on the wrong side of a cowboy's fist."

"Oooooh!" Riley said. He put his hands up in front of his face. "I'm scared." He laughed. "I'll tell you what scared is. Try living in a city. Try riding the subway with the punks and the muggers. These rednecks around here wouldn't have the first clue about making it in the city."

Riley tossed his hair out of his eyes. He looked triumphantly at Judd.

Punch him! That's what he should do, Judd thought. Right now!

3

The Dance at the Legion

Judd clenched his fists. Then he uncurled them. He couldn't punch him out. The Prestons were their friends. His dad had just given him that whole speech at lunch. He sighed.

What his dad had said about Bud and Minnie was true. Judd felt the same way. He would do just about anything for them. Too bad Riley was their grandson.

"So?" Riley said grinning. "Don't you have an answer for that?" He bounced up and down on the motorcycle seat. Dust rose from under the tires.

Riley always tried to make ranch life out as lousy. He put down the valley every chance he had. If his grandparents heard him, they'd be mad. But Judd wasn't going to get hooked into some argument this time.

"Yeah? So what?" Judd said. He shrugged his shoulders. "People around here don't care about the city."

He was interrupted by the sound of hoofbeats. The horses in the corral began to whinny. A voice called from the road. "Judd! Hey, Judd!"

It was Koreene Long. The Longs' ranch was at the end of the valley. Koreene and Judd had grown up together. They had gone to school together since kindergarten. She was like the sister he never had.

They had built lean-tos when they were little. They had fished for tadpoles side by side. He and Koreene had even killed rattlesnakes together. But lately, once in a while, he wondered if they might be more than just good friends.

Koreene rode up on her white horse. She pushed her hat back. Her red hair shone in the sunlight. "Hey, wanna go swimming this afternoon?" she called to Judd.

Before Judd could answer, Riley started the motorcycle. He wheeled around the tree so he could see Koreene.

"Koreene! Hey! How're ya doing?" Riley called. He squeezed the throttle.

VROOOM! VROOOM!

Koreene's horse drew back and whinnied. Koreene pulled up hard on the reins. Tracker barked at Riley.

Koreene frowned. She looked down at Riley from her horse.

"Oh. Hi, Riley. When did you get here?" She stared at the motorcycle. "And what are you doing on *that* thing?"

"This?" Riley asked. He squeezed the throttle again.

VROOOM! VROOOM!

"Hey!" Judd yelled. "Cut it, will you?"

The horses in the corral pawed the ground. Koreene's horse's eyes rolled back. They began to show white. The horse backed away stiff-legged. Tracker barked.

Riley turned the engine off. He made a face. "What a bunch of wimps," he said.

Koreene looked at Judd. She raised her eyebrows. Judd shook his head.

"I can go swimming with you," Riley said. "Even though it's just a dumb pond out in the middle of nowhere. Where I live, the pool..."

"I can't," Judd interrupted. "My dad and I are still mending fences. Once we're finished, we have to clean out the drainage ditches."

"Yeah, I shouldn't really go either," Koreene said. She smiled at Judd. "I have chores to do."

"I get it," Riley said. "Judd's okay. But the city kid

isn't." He looked down at the ground. Then he turned on the engine again.

Koreene looked uncomfortable. She looked as if she actually felt sorry for Riley. Her heart was too soft.

"No. That's not it at all," Koreene responded quickly. "Honestly, it's not."

VROOOM! VROOOM! Riley gunned the engine. He began to roll slowly forward on the motorcycle. He stared down at the front tire.

"Um—Riley," she began again. "Why don't you come with all of us to the dance Friday night? It's at the Legion."

No! Judd wanted to yell. If Riley hated the valley so much, why should they have to ask him to do stuff with them?

"A dance?" Riley asked. He cut the engine. "You mean one of those hoedown things you got up here?" He got his grin back. "Like on *Hee Haw?*"

Judd had gone to the dances at the Legion since he was a baby. In Wells Valley, dances were get-togethers for everyone. All ages came to the dances. Little kids danced and grandpas and grandmas danced. The single people and the cowboys came.

People waltzed and they two-stepped. They square-danced and did the polka. And everyone shared news and gossip. Dances were part of the life of the valley.

Riley was out of line. A hoedown? Judd tightened his mouth. He couldn't believe this guy.

Koreene sighed. "It's not a hoedown thing, Riley. And if you don't want to go, don't come. I was just trying to be nice." She jammed her hat back on her head.

"Okay, okay," Riley said. "Just kidding. Honest." He looked at Koreene. "You're going for sure?"

Koreene nodded.

"I'll come too." Riley turned and grinned at Judd.

"Okay," Koreene said. "A bunch of us are going in my family's truck. We'll pick you up around seven."

Koreene looked at Judd. She smiled. "You too, of course," she said. "Well, gotta go," she finished. She turned her horse and they trotted off.

"Now there's a..." Riley began.

"I gotta finish lunch and get to work," Judd broke in. He didn't want to hear what Riley was going to say about Koreene. He was already angry enough. "See ya," he said. He walked back to the house. The motorcycle roared away.

When Friday night came, Judd was still mad. He had been working hard all week. Meanwhile, Riley had been fooling around. He'd been tearing up the hills.

Judd had heard the obnoxious whine of the motorcycle every day. He could always tell where Riley was by the cloud of dust hanging high in the air.

The Prestons gave Riley a few chores. But they didn't ask him to do many. Riley had a way of wasting time when he was supposed to be working. And then he did such a lousy job that someone usually had to do it over anyway. Judd figured that Riley pretended to be use-less. That way, he wouldn't have to do any work. What a jerk!

When the Longs' truck pulled up, eight kids were packed in the back. Koreene's parents and her grand-mother sat in the king cab. Everyone talked loudly above the noise of the wind.

"Did you hear about the mountain lion tracks?"

"Hey, my old man got a new tractor. I can even..."

"There's gonna be a new eighth-grade teacher in September!"

All the way to the dance, Riley was pretty quiet. But then, everyone else was talking so much. They hadn't all been together since school let out. So Riley really didn't have a chance to brag about anything.

Judd bounced along in the truck. The warm wind whipped through his hair. Even at night, it was still warm. He couldn't remember a summer so hot. He looked at the mountains. They looked black against the early evening sky.

Wednesday, he'd seen Andy at the Wells Valley store buying groceries.

"Haven't seen you in a while," Andy had said. He rolled the cart to the checkout counter.

"Yeah, I've been mending fences," Judd complained. "How are things? What's the news on the fires?"

Andy sighed. "Not good. They've had to call FEMA in for the Northern California fire."

Judd knew those letters stood for a mouthful of words. What were they? He tried to remember. Oh, yeah, they stood for Federal Emergency Management Agency. Whew. Those were top firefighters. They were a last resort.

"Bad, huh?" Judd asked. He juggled a couple of packages of gum while he waited in line.

"Like I've been saying. It's the worst fire season I remember." Andy frowned. "We're just hoping we don't get hit here in the valley," he said. "It would be a disaster."

"We're here!" Koreene said, breaking into Judd's thoughts.

"EEE-HAW!" Riley hollered. He hopped down from the tailgate.

Some of the kids turned to look at him. They exchanged glances. Some of them hid smiles.

Judd knew what they were thinking. Riley's always the same jerk.

Japanese lanterns were strung across the front of the American Legion Hall. Groups of people stood around outside chatting in the night air. Laughter and music poured out of the open double doors.

A wave of sound greeted them when they walked in. Tables had been pushed aside to make room for the dancers. Couples were two-stepping on the dance floor. Little kids danced. Old folks danced. On the raised bandstand, a piano player, a fiddler, and a guitar player pumped out the tune.

Judd saw his parents. His mom gracefully twirled under his dad's arm. Teddy was dancing with somebody's grandma.

"Hey, let's go!" Riley said, grabbing Koreene's arm. He pulled her onto the dance floor. Koreene looked trapped and confused.

Judd folded his arms and watched. Riley did some kind of strange dance. It sure didn't go with the two-step the band was playing. As always, he was making a fool of himself.

Koreene looked over at Judd helplessly. Finally, the song ended.

Riley and Koreene rejoined the group of kids. Riley puffed out his chest. "Anyone seen my new motorcycle?" he asked loudly. He looked at the group. "It's cool." He grinned. "It'll climb any hill."

No one said anything. Several rolled their eyes. Koreene looked down at the floor. She was probably sorry she'd asked Riley along. That'd teach her to feel sorry for an idiot.

"So? Anyone want to try riding it?" Riley asked. "It does exactly what you tell it. Not like a dumb horse."

That did it. Judd turned away. He didn't want to have any part of this. He didn't care what his parents told him. He couldn't be nice to Riley. Riley wouldn't let him.

4

A Visit to the Station

"No way!" Judd said. He slammed the silverware drawer shut.

"That's no way to talk to your mother!" Whit snapped.

The rest of his family sat at the breakfast table. Judd and his father had been up since before daybreak doing chores.

Judd tightened his mouth. "Sorry, Mom," he said, his teeth clenched.

"I just think it would be nice to take Riley with you," his mother said. "Let him get a taste of life here."

Judd was going to the fire station, and his mom was insisting he ask Riley to go.

"It might be good for him to talk with Andy too," Whit said. "Andy might talk some sense into him about that motorcycle."

"I don't think Riley wants a taste of life here," Judd said as he sat down. "And no one can talk any sense into him because he won't listen. And Mom," he said, looking at his mother, "I like talking to Andy and everyone else at the station about fire stuff. Riley won't be interested. He could care less about the valley. All he cares about is his motorcycle. And getting out of Wells Valley."

Teddy spoke up. "I'll take Riley fishing at the pond," he said helpfully.

"That's thoughtful of you, Teddy." Whit smiled at his younger son.

Judd held back a sigh. Whatever Teddy did, his father liked. Teddy *was* a good little kid. Especially for a little brother. But why was he always so perfect?

"Great idea, Teddy," Judd added. "Thanks a lot." All right! Now he could go visit the station without that loser Riley.

Whit went on. His voice was level. "I still think you should take Riley with you, Judd. He needs to know about the fire dangers of riding a motorcycle in dry weather. At least do it for Bud and Minnie."

Judd knew that level tone of voice. He took a deep breath.

"Okay, Dad. I'll ask him to go with me," he said heavily.

He phoned Riley. "You know where the fire station is, right? Well, give me about a 20-minute head start," Judd said. "I don't want your motorcycle spooking Cab on the way."

Judd hung up the phone. He shook his head. "It'd sure be easier if Riley would get on a horse," Judd said. He made a face. "But he won't do it." Judd looked at his family. "He says riding horses is for redneck ranchers. But if you want to know the truth, I think he's scared." Judd grinned a little.

Within ten minutes, Judd was riding Cab next to the road. Her hooves thudded in the dirt and grass. She bobbed her head up and down in time with her steps. Tracker trotted in front of them. His tongue hung from his mouth. It was another hot, dry day.

Judd could see the Wells Valley Fire Station about half a mile ahead. The morning sun flashed on the flagpole. Had FEMA gotten the Northern California fire under control yet? Andy would tell him the latest.

Cab's hooves brushed through the tall, dry grass. Judd mopped his forehead. Not even nine o'clock, and it must be 90 degrees already. He'd get a cool drink at the fire station.

VROOOM! VROOOM!

Cab tossed her head and tried to canter. Tracker barked.

"Whoa, girl! Whoa!" Judd called. He pulled up on the reins.

Riley's motorcycle whined up next to him in the brush. Riley grinned at him and gunned the engine.

"Get outta here!" Judd called angrily.

Cab was trying to toss her head. She began sidestepping. Judd shortened the reins.

"I told you to give me 20 minutes!" he yelled.

Riley grinned. "Sorry. Got bored waiting around in this dump," he hollered. Then he gunned the engine and popped a wheelie. He took off down the side of the road.

Judd watched him get smaller in the distance. He leaned over and patted Cab's neck.

"Sorry, girl," he said. "Guess we'll have to put up with him." He sighed.

When Judd arrived at the fire station, he dismounted. He tied Cab's reins to the hitching post in front. Riley's motorcycle leaned on its kickstand. It shone in the hot sun. Waves of heat rose from it.

Judd walked into the open engine house. Tracker followed, panting. Riley was already there, looking at the shiny, red wildland fire engine.

Riley stared at it. It had knobby off-road tires. A brush, or wildland, engine was used in mountain areas. It was smaller than a regular fire engine. It could go off-road easily.

Sometimes Andy joked about the "Pavement Queens" that the city fire departments used. They were huge, long fire engines with long ladders. They'd never make it in Wells Valley, he said. Mountain and rough terrain fire fighting called for wildland engines.

But the wildland engines couldn't fight the battle alone. Air tankers were used too. Those flew overhead and dropped *phoschek*, a fire retardant. An air attack ship, another plane, would fly with them. It would direct the air tankers so they knew where to drop the phoschek. Bulldozers and choppers were needed too.

"Cool," Riley said as he walked around the engine slowly. His footsteps echoed in the high-ceilinged engine house. "Fires are so cool," he added.

Judd could see Martin, the fire station engineer on this shift, in the cab of the engine. Judd knew he was probably doing the daily log on the mileage. He also had to check how many hours the pump and the engine had run.

At the back of the station, Andy was refilling his canteens. He looked up when he heard Judd's footsteps. He smiled.

"I was wondering when you'd show up," he said. Andy reached down and scratched Tracker between his ears.

Tim and Cord walked out of the station door. "Here he is," Tim joked. "The hotshot of the 21st century!"

"Yeah," Cord echoed. "Got your shovel, little

buddy?"

Judd felt his face turn warm above his shirt collar. They teased him all the time. But it was different in front of Riley.

Riley looked at him. "Hotshot?" he asked. "You wanna be a hotshot?" He smirked.

Tim and Cord became quiet. They looked at each other. Riley never misses a chance to act like a jerk, Judd thought.

"Hey! Hey, dudes!" A voice called from the huge doorway.

Everyone turned to look. At the entrance stood two scruffy-looking guys. They had hair to their shoulders. The taller one had a beard and a headband. Neither had shaved in days. The shorter one wore a huge peace sign on a leather thong around his neck. They both wore sunglasses. Backpacks were slung over their backs, and they carried rolled-up sleeping bags.

Sometimes the valley had some strange visitors. Some people wanted to "get back to nature," as they'd say. They'd camp for a while. But then they'd find life too hard. And they'd move on.

"Hey, dudes, where can we go camping around here?" the taller one asked.

Tracker growled. Andy stepped forward to introduce himself. "I'm Andy Carr," he said, reaching out for a handshake. "We're in the height of fire season right now. So camping is pretty limited.

"You can camp up canyon at the end of this road," Andy continued. He pointed to the road in front of the fire station. "But," he stared at the two, "absolutely no open fires. None. This is the driest we've seen the valley in 25 years," he said.

The shorter of the two looked up at Andy. "We can't cook anything?" he complained. "So how're we gonna eat?"

"You'll have to work that out," Andy said. "Sorry, but we've got a forest and ranches to protect. It's the law, fellas."

"Aw, man, everywhere we go, it's the same," the taller one said. "Government making stupid rules."

"Well, thanks, I guess," the shorter one said. They turned and shuffled back down the driveway.

Andy shook his head. He looked at Martin in the cab. "I think we got ourselves a problem," he said.

"A big one," Martin agreed.

"Hey," Riley nudged Judd. "Let's follow them. We'll catch them cooking. Or smoking dope. Or maybe even starting a fire! Then we can turn them in! We'll have some excitement up here for a change!"

Riley's eyes gleamed. "It'd be cool to watch the fire," Riley added. "Then we could watch Andy and everybody put it out. Maybe you could even be a hotshot," he said, grinning nastily.

Judd stared at Riley. "You just have to make something happen, don't you?" he asked. "A fire's not the kind of excitement we need. And these guys don't need our help with the strangers," Judd said looking at the three firefighters.

Andy looks worried, thought Judd. What does he know that we don't?

5

The Campers

Andy followed the two guys with his eyes. They walked up the road toward the canyon. Andy frowned.

Martin climbed out of the engine cab. "What was that all about?" he asked. "Those two jokers don't think they're gonna cook over an open fire, do they?" He looked at Andy.

Judd was worried. He thought the two strangers looked like they didn't give a hoot about forest fire danger. In fact, they looked as if they couldn't wait to break a rule just because it was there.

Judd's stomach churned. An act of carelessness could cause the valley to become a firestorm. Judd imagined 30- and 40-foot high flames leaping over the ridges. He had seen fires like that on the TV news.

Andy tightened his mouth. "Who knows?" he said. He looked over at Tim and Cord.

"Hey, fellas," he said. "I'm putting you two in charge. Find where they're camping. Then drive up there in the station Jeep a couple of times a day. Just to keep an eye on 'em. You know. Especially around mealtime. All right? I'll tell Pete when his shift comes in Monday."

"You bet," Tim said. "I'd like to bust those two losers for H and S code 13001."

"Yeah," Cord echoed. "I'd just like to bust 'em period. Were they running an attitude, or what?" he asked Andy. "Sheesh!"

Riley looked at Andy. "What's an 'H and S code 13001'?" he asked.

"Health and Safety code. It's a state law in California," Andy explained. "If you start a fire accidentally, you violate section 13001." Andy frowned. "Fire Investigation sends some guys out. Then the person is arrested."

Riley looked interested. "Does he go to jail?" he asked Andy.

"No," Andy said. "H and S 13001 is accidental fire. It's a misdemeanor. Not like arson. That's on purpose. It's a felony."

Andy continued. "But anyone who violates H and S 13001 has to pay a big fine and is put on probation."

Andy looked back at Tim and Cord. "I want you on those two creeps like stink on a hog," he said. "Got it?"

Tim and Cord grinned. "You bet," Cord said.

"With pleasure," Tim agreed.

"Hey," Riley said. "Anyone wanna see my new motorcycle?" He looked at the group.

Jeez, Judd thought. Riley always had to be the center of attention. This was getting old. Riley hadn't even been in the valley a week, and Judd was tired of him already.

Andy turned to Riley. "You bet. Let's see this motorcycle," he said kindly.

Andy, Riley, and Judd walked out of the station toward the dirt bike. It gleamed in the sun. "You have a spark arrester on it, right?" Andy asked.

Riley looked down at the ground. "Ah, well, I have one. I took it off."

Andy frowned. "You'd better..." he began.

"Yeah, don't worry. I know," Riley said quickly. "At home, it's kinda cool to have the bike sound noisy. I'll put it back on. I promise. I just forgot. Honest."

Riley was such a fool. He shouldn't be riding a motorcycle anywhere without a spark arrester. And especially not here in the valley.

Andy stared at Riley. "You put that spark arrester back on today. I'll red-tag your bike if you don't. You'll be walking everywhere. Sorry to take such a hard line.

But," he gestured at the dry, brown hills around them, "there's a lot at stake."

"Yeah, okay. No problem. See?" Riley said, changing the subject. He pointed to his bike. "It's an XL200. It's about ten years old. But it's a classic dirt bike."

Riley bragged about the bike while they checked it out. Then they all walked back into the engine house.

"Don't you forget about that spark arrester, son," Andy said.

"I won't," Riley answered.

Right, Judd thought.

"Well, gotta go," Riley said. He made a face. "The grandparents have a chore list a mile long for me. They think I'm their personal slave or something," he complained.

Judd saw Tim and Cord roll their eyes. Andy hid a smile.

"So long," Riley said. He turned and walked back down the driveway. Then he stopped. "Hey, Vandorf," he called.

Judd looked back at Riley.

"I'll be by later. We'll talk about our plan. Okay?" Riley asked.

Great. Just what he wanted—to see Riley again today. "Maybe," Judd said.

Plan? Judd puzzled. What was Riley talking about? Oh, yeah. That dumb plan to spy on the campers.

Judd had no desire to spend any more time with

Riley. Judd had taken him to the station—just like his parents wanted. But now he was finished with Riley. For today anyway.

They heard the motorcycle engine sputter and then catch. The noise whined away, echoing against the hills.

"What a piece of work that kid is," Tim said.

"Aw, he's just lonely," Andy said. "Give him a break."

Lonely! Judd thought. That's because he's such a jerk. No one *wants* to be around him. That's why he's lonely!

"He'd better put that spark arrester on, though," Andy added.

"Lazy S calling Wells Valley Fire Station. Lazy S calling Wells Valley Fire Station." The CB radio crackled through the air. It echoed in the fire station.

Martin and Andy looked at each other.

Was it a fire? Judd's heart raced, even though he knew that the ranchers would be more likely to call 911 for a fire. Then the fire dispatcher would call in the first alarm fire from 911 right to the station. But the ranchers might use the CB. Especially if they were out on the ranch somewhere. You never knew.

Martin hustled to the CB.

"Wells Valley Fire Station here. Over," he said.

Static punctuated the voice on the CB. "Wells Valley Fire Station, this is the Lazy S. Ralph here. How're you boys doing out there? Hot enough for ya yet? Over," the voice joked.

Judd relaxed. It was just Ralph Ward at the Lazy S.

Martin grinned. "No, not yet. What can we do for ya? Over," he said.

The voice faded in and out a bit. "We got some cattle wanderin' over the road here. They got the Circle K brand on 'em. You wanna hail down the Circle K? Must have some fence down. Over."

"Thanks, Ralph. We'll call 'em," Martin said. "Over and out." He let go of the mike button.

There was always something going on at the fire station. "Hey," Judd said. "I'll ride by the Circle K if you want."

"We'll call 'em on the phone," Andy said. "But if you want to go by, go ahead. They'd probably be glad for a little help getting the cattle back in." He looked at everyone. "Every time that CB goes on, I gotta tell you, I worry."

"Uh-huh," Martin agreed.

Andy looked out the window at the golden hills. "It doesn't get much worse than this. First, we have so much rain that everything grows like crazy. Then we don't get any rain for six months. Too much dry fuel to burn out there. I've never seen a summer like this one."

Andy turned back from the window. "It feels like we're living in a tinderbox, doesn't it?" He shook his head.

"Yeah," Martin said. "I keep waking up at night thinking I smell smoke."

"Well, we're ready," Andy said. "If we get hit, we're ready." He frowned. "We've gotta keep an eye on those two jokers up canyon, though. Tim? Cord?"

Tim and Cord looked at Andy. They nodded.

Then Andy looked at Judd. "You keep a lookout too, all right? While you're out riding around, watch for any possible problems—anything that might start a fire. You know, downed power lines, that kind of thing."

"Sure!" Judd said quickly. "You bet." He grinned at Andy.

He felt proud. Andy had asked for his help. It was almost like being part of the team. Of course, he'd watch for fires, even if Andy hadn't asked him. He didn't want a firestorm to savage the valley.

6
Where's Riley Going?

The rest of Saturday passed quietly. Judd helped the Baxters at the Circle K round up their stray cattle. He left Mr. Baxter mending the section of fence with the help of his son Bobby and the hired hand.

Late in the afternoon, Judd was out in the corral. He was cleaning Cab's hooves. He hadn't seen Tracker in a while. He's probably off in the hills somewhere hunting something, Judd thought.

VROOOM! VROOOM!

Judd jumped. That darn Riley. This was not the time to spook Cab. It was tricky enough cleaning hooves.

Judd set Cab's hoof down. Reaching up, he patted her neck. "It's all right, girl," he said.

Cab quivered a little. But she stood still.

"Gettin' used to that jerk, huh?" he asked her. "I wish I could."

Sure enough, Riley pulled into the yard. This time, he cut the engine early. The bike coasted in.

"Hey, Vandorf," he called. "What's up?"

The sky, you idiot, Judd was tempted to answer. He bit his tongue. Riley was trying, anyway. He had cut the engine a little earlier this time.

"Nothing," Judd said. He waited impatiently. What did Riley want anyway?

Riley rolled the bike closer. Cab shifted her weight nervously. Judd patted her again.

"Steady, girl," he said. Cab blew through her nostrils.

"Hey, how about our plan?" Riley asked. He grinned secretly.

"What plan?" Judd asked. Maybe if he acted like he'd forgotten, Riley would lose interest.

Riley frowned. "Don't you remember?" he asked. "Spying on the campers. We'll catch them doing something. We'll be heroes."

Judd shook his head. "That's crazy, Riley. Tim and Cord can take care of those guys. Plus, how would you get up there? Your dirt bike makes too much noise."

Judd glanced down at the bike. The exhaust pipe was still bare. "Did you put the spark arrester on it yet, like Andy wanted?"

Riley colored above his collar. "Naw, not yet. I will, though. I just forgot." He tossed his hair out of his eyes. "Anyway, I can park my bike at the end of the trail. Then we can walk up canyon. Quietly, of course." He grinned at Judd. "How about it?" he asked. "Wanna be a hero?"

"Nope. 'Fraid not," Judd said. He leaned back against the corral fence. "Tim and Cord will take care of 'em."

"You never want to do anything," Riley complained. "Everyone around this dump is so boring."

Judd clenched his teeth. He was tempted to show Riley some excitement. He'd love to send Riley flying off his bike and into the dirt. What a sight that would be. Judd sighed. Too bad he had to be nice to this jerk.

"Knock it off, Riley," he said. He turned back to Cab. Judd reached down into the bucket. He squeezed a sponge of water over Cab's back. He couldn't finish cleaning her hooves until the motorcycle was gone. But he could wash and scrape her.

"Sick. How can you do all that stuff?" Riley asked. He grimaced.

"Don't you take care of your motorcycle?" Judd asked over his shoulder.

"Yeah. Well, pretty much," he said. "I change the oil. Sometimes I have to adjust the chain. That kind of stuff."

"Same thing," Judd said. "Your bike won't run

without it, right?"

Riley nodded.

"Well, Cab needs all that too. If I don't do it, no one else will," he said. He sponged Cab. Then he got the scraper. He began scraping her sides.

"Gross," Riley said, watching the froth of dirt and horse hair dribble down Cab's sides. "Well, dirt bikes are better than horses any day," he said. "Too bad you won't come with me. Finding those creeps starting a fire will be great. When you read about me in the paper, remember you had your chance."

He grinned and started the engine. Cab tossed her head.

"Settle," Judd said to her.

Riley zoomed out of the yard. A cloud of dust trailed after him.

****

The next morning, Judd sat at the breakfast table. His dad had just finished eating. He pushed his chair away from the table. Judd could hear Teddy outside. "Are we going to church?" Judd asked.

The Vandorfs belonged to the little community church. Most valley people went there, no matter what religion they were. The nearest big town with any churches was Harvey. And that was an hour away.

"To skip an hour's drive, I'll be any religion on Sunday," Judd's dad always joked.

Church was okay. Judd enjoyed seeing his friends there. He'd like to skip the sermon, though. And it was so hot inside the church during the summer. And this summer was hotter than ever.

"Yes," Whit answered. "Eat up and get ready. Then after lunch, your mother and I are going over to the Wards' for some cards. We'll stay for supper. You too."

"You and Teddy can come over later," his mother said. "We'll eat about six or so."

Judd was relieved. Sometimes his dad wanted to do ranch work on Sunday afternoons. He was glad they had other plans.

Supper at the Wards' would be fun. Bobby Ward was a year younger than Judd. Then there were three other younger Ward boys.

Too bad they weren't going to the Longs'. He wouldn't mind seeing Koreene. His stomach gave a funny flip.

As the Vandorfs rode home from church, Judd watched the sky. He scanned the mountainsides for any signs of smoke. Nothing. No fires. Tim and Cord must be watching those two yokels pretty closely. He hoped so.

Judd helped with the dishes after lunch. "Thanks," his mother said. She took a macaroni salad out of the refrigerator.

"We're leaving now," she said. She looked at Judd. "Be careful and watch Teddy. Then the two of you come on over around five or so. Earlier is fine too." She smiled at Judd.

"Oh! I almost forgot," Judd's mother added. She walked to the wall by the phone. She pulled a piece of paper off the bulletin board. She handed Judd a list.

"At church the Prestons said they were going into Harvey later this afternoon," she said. "They're going in for supplies. We need some things. Can you run this list by their place, please?" she asked. She rummaged in her purse. "And here's some money for them," she said. She handed him some bills.

Judd had seen Bud and Minnie at church. But no Riley. He sure hadn't missed him.

"Sure, Mom," he said. Too bad. Now he might have to see Riley. Things had been peaceful without him. Riley'd probably start bugging him about spying on the two campers.

"If Riley's there, ask him to do something with you," Arella suggested.

Right, Judd thought. Not in *this* lifetime.

Whit and Arella drove down the dirt road. The Jeep disappeared.

"Teddy," Judd called out the back door. "I'm going over to Prestons'. Gotta give 'em this list."

"Okay!" Teddy hollered. He was out with the dogs in the pasture.

Judd saddled up Cab. Tracker trotted over. He whined.

"Yes, Track. You can come too. Even though it's your

favorite person," Judd joked.

He rode over to the Prestons'. Tracker led the way. Bud and Minnie were walking out their back door when he rode up.

"Ho!" Judd halted Cab. She snorted, smelling the Prestons' horses. They whinnied to her. One came trotting up to the fence. He blew through his nostrils. Cab nickered.

"Hi, Judd," Bud Preston said. He smiled. "I bet you have a list for us."

"Uh-huh," Judd said. He walked Cab over to their truck.

"You're just in time," Minnie said. "We were just ready to leave for your place. We thought we'd have to stop by to get the list."

"Sorry," Judd said. He took the list out of his pocket. Then he got the money out. He handed them to Bud.

"Why don't you come on in?" Bud said. "Riley'd be glad for some company."

He looked at Minnie. She pressed her mouth together in a thin line.

Uh-oh, Judd thought. Trouble with Riley again. What a surprise.

"I'm surprised Riley isn't going with you," Judd said. "I thought he liked to go into town."

"He just woke up," Minnie said. "He wasn't trying to hurry. And we have to get going before everything closes up. So we told him we'd have to leave without him."

Was there a tone of disgust in her voice?

Bud sighed. "Yep. I don't think that boy's cut out for ranch life," he said.

"Well, if his own parents didn't..." Minnie began. Her color rose.

Bud walked over to her. He put his arm around her.

"Now, Minnie," he said. "Calm down." He looked at Judd. "We'll drop the supplies over on our way home."

"Thanks a lot," Judd said.

The Prestons drove off in a trail of dust. Dogs followed barking.

Riley opened the screen door. He stuck his head out. He was still in the cutoff sweats he slept in.

"Hey," he said crossly. He rubbed his eyes. "What're you doing here?"

"Just brought a list over for your grandparents," Judd said.

"Them," Riley snorted. "Come on in. I was just gonna get dressed. Then I was thinking about a ride in the hills. Wanna come? Maybe we can rustle up a little fun around this boring place."

Sure, Judd thought. Spook Cab. Scare cattle. And get the ranchers ticked off at him.

"No, thanks," he said aloud. "I got stuff to do around the ranch."

"Everybody's always too busy to have fun around here," Riley complained. "Or too busy to wait." He kicked the door. "My own grandparents wouldn't even wait for me to get dressed." He frowned. "A trip to town would have been great. Better than sticking around this dump. I almost wish it were time for school so I could get outta here."

So do I, Judd thought. But he forced himself to keep quiet.

"Where are you going to ride?" Judd asked.

"Oh, nowhere in particular," Riley answered. "Just somewhere up in the hills. Anything's better than hanging around here all day."

Judd turned Cab around. "See ya," he called over his shoulder.

"Yeah," Riley called sullenly.

7
Smoke!

As he rode off, Judd heard Riley slam the screen door. Boy, he's in a bad mood, thought Judd.

Cab's hooves thudded on the dirt road. Puffs of dust rose up with each hoofbeat. Tracker trotted ahead. He panted loudly.

It was awfully hot. The sun burned above Judd, a white-hot disc in the blue sky. He wiped his forehead with the back of his hand.

Back home, Judd groomed Cab and put her away. Teddy was out in the yard with the dogs.

Judd decided to go inside and listen to some CDs. It was too hot to do much outside. He hated to have Cab out in weather this hot for no reason.

Judd slid a CD into the player. He thumbed through a copy of *Sports Illustrated.* Judd's thoughts turned to Riley.

Even though Riley was a pain, Judd couldn't help feeling sorry for him. It was clear Riley hated the valley. He was always complaining about hick ranchers.

His own parents didn't like him. They were always sending him away. And now even his grandparents were getting fed up with him. If Riley couldn't live with his parents, and he couldn't live with his grandparents...

Judd blinked. Wait. Was Riley planning to run away?

Judd sighed. He decided he'd better call and check on Riley. He didn't like the guy, but he didn't want him to run away. And he knew the Prestons would feel terrible.

The Prestons' phone rang and rang. No one answered.

Great. So much for spending the day inside. Judd knew what he had to do. Before jumping to any more conclusions, he'd see if Riley had gone up canyon. He might be spying on the two campers.

Twenty minutes later, Judd rode out of the Bar Vee.

Tracker followed. The air was still and hot.

"Ho!" Judd called to Cab. He pulled up short on the reins. What was that? Did he smell something? He sniffed the air. Tracker whined a little.

Smoke! Judd's heart thudded. Oh, no! Smoke!

"Do you smell it too?" Judd asked Tracker.

Quickly, Judd scanned the hills and the mountains beyond. There! On the hillside! A thin wisp of white smoke twisted into the air.

It was up canyon from the fire station. Judd stared at the mountains. That's probably where those two creeps are camping, Judd thought.

Judd wheeled Cab around and began galloping back to the ranch. He galloped down the dirt road leading to the ranch house. He slid off Cab and tied her to the rail.

He raced up the porch steps. "Teddy! Teddy! Fire!" he yelled as he ran.

Judd grabbed the phone off the wall. He pressed 911. He was dizzy with fear.

Teddy rushed in. His eyes were wide with fright. His face was flushed. "What? Fire?"

"Shhhh!" Judd motioned to him. He was talking to the dispatcher.

"It's up canyon from the valley road. Yes, ranches are threatened....livestock, uh-huh...yes, the firefighters at Wells Valley Fire Station know the area. They may already be there. Okay. Thanks!" Judd hung up the phone.

"We gotta call the other ranches," he told Teddy.

"We'll use the CB in case they're out somewhere."

"A fire? Our ranch might burn?" Teddy asked. He looked worried.

"Don't worry, buddy. It's still pretty far from here. The firefighters know what to do. I'll call Andy just to touch base," Judd said. He had to act calm.

He called the fire station. "Yeah. Yeah....uh-huh. Okay. You bet. Bye," he said.

"What? What?" Teddy asked.

"Andy said they just got the call from fire dispatch. It was my call!" Judd said, a little proudly. "So Andy called in everything."

"What's 'everything'?" Teddy asked.

"Oh, the usual stuff," Judd said. He grabbed a thermos from the cupboard.

"What usual stuff?" Teddy asked.

"Two air tankers for dropping fire retardant. An air attack plane for directing the air tankers," Judd answered as he ran water into the thermos.

"Wow! It sounds like the whole Air Force!" Teddy said. "What about guys and trucks?" he asked.

"Uh-huh," Judd said. "Two bulldozers and two hot-shot crews should be on their way too. And a battalion fire chief comes too."

"No water?" Teddy asked.

He almost forgot! "Oh, yeah! Five other wildland fire engines and three patrols. Those are pickups with pumpers. Sometimes they'll bring in helicopters to dump water."

Teddy's eyes widened even more. "All that stuff? Right away?" he asked.

"You bet," Judd said. "All that's automatic for brush fires. And forest fires. Which I hope we're not gonna have," he added.

"What can we do?" Teddy asked.

"We'll get on the CB. We'll call everyone in the valley," Judd said.

First, Judd tried his parents. But he couldn't get through to the Wards. Judd felt his stomach tighten. Where were the Wards and his parents? Why didn't they have the CB with them? He'd have to try again later.

Judd called the rest of the ranchers. He began to feel as if he were playing a tape over and over again. Each CB call was the same.

The ranchers were worried. They were grateful Judd had called, though. Koreene had answered the phone at the Longs'.

"I'm scared, Judd," Koreene had said. "My parents are in town. Over."

Judd was surprised. Koreene wasn't afraid of anything. But a fire was frightening. He was scared too. At least their ranch wasn't threatened yet. The fire had to burn down canyon first. Then the Prestons' ranch would be first to burn.

"My parents are gone too. If the fire comes closer your way, I'll call you. Over," Judd assured her.

"But the ranch house!" Koreene wailed. "I'm worried

our house will burn down! Over."

"Turn on your irrigation system," Judd said. "All your sprinklers. Everywhere. In all the pastures. Wet your roof down with a hose. That's what I'm gonna do. He frowned. "Oh, and Koreene. Is the brush cleared away from your house? Over."

Koreene said her dad had just cleared the 30-foot swath around the house again last week. Most ranchers were pretty good about getting that done.

Judd signed off the CB. He had tried the Prestons', but no one was there. They must not have taken the CB with them in the truck. And still no Riley.

Teddy was staring out the window, his nose pressed against the glass. "Oh, no, Judd," Teddy's voice quavered. "It looks like it's getting bigger," he said.

Judd joined him. He looked out at the mountains. Sure enough, the wisp of white smoke had grown to a plume.

Judd scanned the sky for the air tankers. None yet. In the distance, he could hear sirens. This was really happening. He wished he could help the firefighters.

"Don't worry, Teddy," Judd said. He tried to act calm. "Andy said he'd call if we had to evacuate. He said with the light wind, it'll burn maybe ten or so acres an hour. We have time. We have a couple of hours—maybe three—at least. We're not in danger yet."

"Okay," Teddy said. He looked a little pale.

"First, let's go turn on the irrigation," Judd said.

"Let's get everything wet down."

They raced down the porch steps to the barn. The smell of smoke hung in the air. It was a bitter smell. Judd shivered despite the heat.

Was Fire Investigation already on their way? Those two campers would be in big trouble if they had anything to do with this.

The campers. Wait—Riley! Judd suddenly remembered that Riley had been going to look for the campers. Oh, no! What if Riley were up there too?

Riley was just the type to be careless enough to watch the fire burn. He was always looking for excitement. "Fires are cool," Riley had said.

But fire was not a spectator sport. It was dangerous.

Should he try to find Riley? Judd's mouth was dry. Riley must be up there. He probably went to spy on the campers.

Judd had no choice. He could never forgive himself if Riley got hurt. He could never meet the Prestons' eyes again. He could already see their stricken faces if something happened to Riley.

"I'm gonna see if I can't find where Riley went," Judd told Teddy. "He might get trapped by the flames. He doesn't know anything about fires. He probably thinks it's cool to be right in the middle of things."

"Don't be gone too long, Judd," Teddy said. He looked worried.

Judd punched Teddy's shoulder lightly. "Don't

worry, bro. I'll be back in less than an hour. We've got time. Hours, in fact.

"Mom and Dad will be home soon," Judd added. "You can start watering down the roof. I've gotta find Riley, though. Before something happens to him. I gotta tell Andy he's out there too," he added.

Judd's boots thumped down the steps. He jumped on Cab's back. He kicked her into a canter. Tracker took off like a shot, following.

"Let's go, girl. We gotta find your favorite person," he told Cab.

Judd rode out under the front gate of the Bar Vee. The smell of smoke was everywhere. The breeze was picking up. Now the bright blue sky was fading to a smoky gray above the fire.

Riley. That jerk. Was he watching the fire burn? Was he going to get trapped by the flames up canyon?

8

It's Heading for the Prestons'!

Distant sirens screamed. Now Judd could hear aircraft. He squinted his eyes. Yes. There was the air attack plane. It swooped down low. It was checking out the fire.

Judd cantered Cab up away from the road. He tried to follow the trail Riley might have taken. He could see the tire tracks of Riley's XL200. Were the tracks made today?

No sense in going by the station. Andy wouldn't be there anyway. He'd be up at the fire line.

Judd's arm brushed by tree branches. He almost lost his hat once. Cab's steady canter carried him closer to the fire. Tracker trotted next to Cab.

Judd could hear more sirens. Engines throbbed in the distance.

Bulldozers growled faintly. They must already be clearing the brush away from the fire's path. Andy told him the key to stopping a fire was not letting it have anything to burn. So bulldozers cleared a path on either side of the fire. Then they tried to pinch it off in front.

The hotshot crews cleared the forest too. They used pulaskis and shovels. *Pulaskis* were tools that were half hoe and half ax. They were used to chop the brush and small trees.

Judd was close enough to hear voices. The air was thick with smoke. It burned the inside of his nose. It stung his eyes. But his heart pounded with excitement. Someday, this was going to be his life.

There! Through the trees, he could see the command post. They always set up at the beginning of a fire. The anchor point, Andy called it.

Firefighters in yellow Nomex fire shirts and pants hurried everywhere. They called to each other.

Tables sat near the trucks. Equipment covered them. Radios and computers sat on them. Screens were lit. It was like a battle headquarters.

Patrols pumped water. Wildland engines rolled toward the flames. From where he sat on Cab, he could see smaller flames still burning. Guys were putting them out.

Most of the action was up ahead. The firefighters were working to stop the fire before it burned down to the valley. Good thing fire burned slower downhill.

Judd saw Andy. He slipped off Cab and tied her with a slip knot to a tree. She quivered a little. Tracker whined a little.

"Don't worry, Cab," he said. "You're not going any closer. I know it's too much excitement for you." He patted her neck. He made his way toward Andy. Tracker followed.

Andy was talking to three people, two men and a woman. They had clipboards. They looked serious.

Wait! The campers were there too. Were they being charged?

Judd walked closer.

"So, you've been up here since yesterday?" the woman was asking. She was taking notes on her clipboard.

These people must be Fire Investigation. They came to the scene of a fire immediately. Then when things cooled down, they traced the burn pattern. In this way, they found exactly where the fire started.

Next, Fire Investigation would stake out the area in a grid. They took days to sift each square foot. Andy said they could find anything that way. Cigarette butts, matches, or anything that could start a fire. They were experts.

Judd looked at the two campers. The bearded one looked mad. The other one looked worried.

I'd be plenty worried if I were them, Judd thought. Imagine starting a forest fire like this. What a couple of jerks.

"Don't you guys think about going anywhere," one of the men said. He looked at the two campers threateningly.

"Cool it, dude," the bearded guy said. "We're tellin' ya. We didn't start it. I swear. We didn't do any cooking."

"That's right," the other one said. "We didn't start any fire. Honest." He still looked worried.

"Well, let's hope you're telling the truth," the other man said. He looked disgusted.

"Call me if you need me," Andy told the investigators. "I'll be here." Andy turned to join the men at the computer screens.

Then Andy saw Judd standing under a live oak tree. "Hey!" Andy called. He walked up to Judd. "What are you doing here?" he asked. He tipped his brush helmet back.

Judd hoped Andy wasn't mad at him for coming up. "Ah, I came to tell you Riley's missing," he said quickly.

"Missing?" Andy asked. "What do you mean, missing?" He mopped his forehead with a bandanna.

It was hot here. Hot and smoky. Voices shouted to each other. Engines throbbed. Dozers chugged over the ridge.

"He's not at the Prestons'," Judd said. "He took off somewhere on his motorcycle. He was pretty mad. I think he might have run away, or..."

"That poor kid is nothing but trouble," Andy broke in. "But why'd you come up here in the middle of the fire to tell me that? I've got other, more important things to do."

"I'm afraid he might have gone up to spy on the campers," Judd said. "I'm afraid he might be up there watching the fire burn. You know how he likes excitement." Judd looked at Andy worriedly.

"Oh, great," Andy groaned. "Just what I need. A civilian in the middle of my fire. And he's definitely the wrong kind of civilian." Andy shook his head.

"So, I thought you'd better know," Judd said.

"Yeah, you're right," Andy said. "I'll pass the word down the fire line." He sighed. "Riley Preston equals trouble."

"Thanks, Andy," Judd said.

"You did the right thing," Andy said. "Thanks." He smiled at Judd.

"Good luck," Judd said. "See ya." He waved and began jogging back to Cab. Tracker ran alongside him, tail wagging.

Judd hated to leave all the excitement. But he had to. Fire lines were no place for civilians.

The trees began to rustle with a stronger breeze. Oh, no, Judd thought. Wind would only make the flames higher and hotter.

He swung up onto Cab. He turned her. He looked across the ridge. Trees were torching out, as Andy called it.

Trees caught fire from the burning grass. They burned from the bottom up. The trunk caught fire first. Then leaves and twigs flickered into flame. Then the whole tree exploded into a flaming torch. It took less than a minute for the whole tree to torch out.

Judd looked down the valley. The flames were marching down faster than he thought they would. His stomach tightened. The Prestons' ranch lay right in the fire's path. In another hour or two, their place would be in danger. Then his place.

Judd kicked Cab into a canter. "Let's go, girl," he said. "We gotta get to the Prestons'."

Cab cantered furiously through the trees. Her hooves thudded in the dirt and dry grass. Tracker streaked through the grass.

Thankfully, people in the valley didn't lock their doors. He could get into the Prestons'. He'd call the fire station from there and check on the speed of the fire.

Judd knew what he'd do when and if the fire got close. First, he'd unlatch the gates. He'd turn the animals loose. He'd call Teddy and tell him to do the same at their place. Then he'd race for their ranch.

The Prestons' ranch came into view. Judd checked the yard. No motorcycle. Riley was still missing.

Judd tied up Cab and raced into the house. He made his call to the fire station. Then grabbing the CB, he ran outside.

The white and gray smoke was billowing into the sky now. Little burned bits of leaves and cinders were drifting to the ground. His eyes stung from the smoke.

Judd looked around him. He checked where all the gates were. He ran to the barn and turned on their irrigation system. Wetting everything down would help. Back outside again, he stared at the house.

Thankfully, the Prestons had cleared brush away 30 feet from the house. But past that, plenty of fuel waited for the hungry flames. The dry brush and grass rustled in the breeze.

Did he have time? He stared up canyon. On the hillside, tongues of flame leaped up through the smoke. He shuddered.

If he could disc a firebreak farther away, the house might be saved. His dad had cleared almost 75 feet of brush away from their house. It had been a lot of work. But, as Whit said, it would definitely be worth it if a fire came.

The tractor sat by the side of the barn. The disker was attached. Judd jumped up, set the CB on the seat, and started up the tractor. The motor chugged. Yes! he thought. Good thing he'd been driving a tractor since he was Teddy's age.

He rounded the side of the barn on the tractor. Just as he drove around the corner, he heard it. VROOOM! VROOOM!

9
Fire!

Judd felt a wave of relief wash over him. For once, he was actually happy to see Riley.

Judd let the tractor motor idle. He stood up.

"Hey!" he yelled. "Hey!"

Riley looked across the yard. He looked surprised to see Judd.

Riley rode the motorcycle over. The engine sputtered and coughed.

"I thought it was Grandpa on the tractor," he said. His face was drained of color. "What's happening? Is the fire coming?"

Well, at least he has enough sense to be scared, Judd thought.

"Yes, it's coming," Judd shouted over the noise of the tractor. "Where have you been?"

"Just riding around," he said. "Wh-what can we do?"

"I'm gonna clear a bigger fire break," Judd hollered. "Grab an ax from the barn. That's all you've got. Start chopping down stuff."

Riley turned off the motorcycle and raced for the barn.

Judd began disking the brush. It was slow work. Every now and then, he stared up at the smoke and the flames.

Was it his imagination? Or were they coming closer? He kept listening for the crackle of the CB radio. They'd promised they'd call him.

Teddy! He almost forgot! He set the tractor on a straight course. He called his house.

"Teddy. It's Judd. Over," he said. He steered the tractor with one hand.

Teddy's voice squeaked over the air. "Judd! Where are you? I'm scared! Over," Teddy said.

"Over at the Prestons'. Have you heard from Mom and Dad? Over," he said.

"Yeah. They decided to go into town with the Wards.

But they heard about the fire. It's all over the news. They're on their way home. But when are you coming? Over," the trembling voice asked.

"I'm clearing a firebreak," Judd said. "The brush is pretty close to the house here. Then we'll clear some things out that the Prestons might want saved. We'll let the animals loose when the station calls. Then I'll be home.

"Don't worry," Judd continued. "We've got a couple hours still. The station'll call in plenty of time. They always do. Did you get everything wet down? Over," Judd said.

"Yeah, I did it. Just like you said," Teddy said. Judd heard him sniffle across the airwaves. "Hurry up. Over."

"See ya, kid. Over," Judd finished. Both hands on the wheel now, he turned the tractor. Back it chugged, the disker churning up brush and dirt behind it.

Off ahead of him, Riley was swinging the ax. He whacked at bushes and small trees.

Riley's face looked white and drawn. So city life was tough, huh? He bet Riley was sure changing his mind.

AAARRRRRR! AAARRRRR!

Sirens came closer. Judd heard the chugging of the dozers. They moved closer too.

The CB crackled. "Wells Valley Fire Station to Prestons. Wells Valley Fire Station to Prestons. Over."

Judd's heart thudded. This was it. He idled the tractor. He pushed in the mike button on the CB.

"Judd Vandorf for the Preston Ranch. I hear you. Over," he said. He tried to sound calm.

"You must evacuate. Repeat. You must evacuate. Over," the voice commanded.

"Okay. We're outta here. Over," Judd said. He shut off the tractor.

Grabbing the CB, he hollered to Riley, "Let's go! Let the animals out. Get your stuff. Unlock the gates. Hurry!"

In a frenzy, the two boys unlatched gates. They slapped the horses' rumps.

"Go on! Get outta here!" they yelled.

The smell of smoke was already making the horses nervous. They took off across the open fields away from the flames. Cattle were already bunched at the far gate in terror. They began taking off in their funny, loping gait.

Riley rushed into the house. He came out a few moments later carrying a backpack. "Grandma's silver, some old pictures, and some of my stuff," he explained to Judd.

He shouldered the backpack and headed toward his motorcycle.

"You can't ride that," Judd said firmly. "There's too much fire danger. Get on the back of Cab."

Judd wheeled Cab around. Dust rose from under her hooves.

Riley backed away a few steps. "I-I don't do much riding. Horses are dumb," he said. He tossed his head.

"Look, this dumb horse is gonna save your life. Now

get on. We need to hurry!" Judd snapped.

Judd reached down with one hand and helped pull Riley up. Riley held onto the back of his shirt.

"Giddap, Cab," Judd said, kicking her into a gallop. "Hold on!" he yelled back to Riley.

They raced for the Vandorfs, a half-mile away. Tracker ran on ahead. Poor Teddy, Judd thought. He must be in a panic.

Cab's hooves drummed on the dirt. The sky was gray and smoky. Ashes and cinders drifted down almost like snowflakes.

The smoky air burned the back of Judd's throat and singed his nose. It was so hot. Even the wind was hot. Behind them, the wind fed the flames.

Cab galloped into the Vandorfs' yard. All across the pasture, the sprinklers were running. Teddy ran down the porch steps.

"Judd! Judd!" he yelled. "Is it coming? Is the fire coming?"

"Not yet, Teddy. But we have to be ready," Judd said.

In the distance, he could hear the dozers. Please, please, cut the fire off, he begged.

In the ranch house, Teddy had piled up some things to take with them. Judd went over them. His grandfather's watch, his grandmother's pin, some pictures, Dad's important papers in his leather case.

"When are Mom and Dad coming?" Teddy asked. He looked worriedly at Judd.

"I'll bet they'll be here any minute," Judd said. He hoped so anyway.

Riley stood at the window. He stared at the smoke billowing up. "How will we know if my place is burning?" he asked.

"Once the smoke turns black. That means a building is burning," Judd said. "As long as it's white and gray, it's just forest and brush." Just, he thought. All those beautiful trees. The hills.

"I hope those dumb campers have learned their lesson," Judd burst out. "I'd like to deck 'em for starting this. Wouldn't you?" he asked Riley. "Especially if your ranch goes."

"Yeah," Riley said slowly. He didn't turn around. He just stared out the window. Judd joined him.

"How long have we got?" Teddy asked. He tugged on Judd's sleeve.

"It depends on how hard the wind blows," Judd said. "It could be another hour before we have to evacuate." His stomach tightened. Evacuate. It was so final. The end. No more ranch.

In the sky, Judd watched the air tankers dropping the phoschek. Big plumes of it cascaded to the earth below.

Andy had even called in a couple of choppers. They swung huge buckets of water. They dumped the hundreds of gallons of water on the flames below. Then they flew back to the reservoir five miles away for more water.

Water! He had to water the roof down again. "Riley,

grab the hose," Judd called.

Judd raced out to the barn and got a second hose. He hooked his hose up to a faucet.

Riley and Judd worked together to water both sides of the roof.

Water drops glistened in the sun. But cinders and ashes kept falling from the sky. Judd watched carefully. He didn't want any burning embers landing anywhere. So far, so good. His heart raced.

Suddenly, Teddy burst through the screen door outside.

"Hey! The fire station just called!" he yelled at them. "It's under control! They stopped it!"

A huge wave of relief washed over Judd.

"Yes!" he cheered. He threw the hose up in the air. Water sprayed everywhere. "Way to go, Andy!"

Teddy jumped up and down. "Yay!" he hollered. "We're safe!"

Judd glanced at Riley. He didn't look very excited. In fact, he looked pale.

10
The Burn Pattern

An hour later, the Prestons' truck pulled up in the yard.

"Riley! Your grandparents are here!" Teddy yelled.

Judd's parents walked around the side of the house. They had come home right after the fire station called.

Judd and Riley came in from the deck. They had been watching the smoke from the fire.

The sound of dozers droned in the distance. Just one air tanker flew overhead. The smoke was thinning out.

Still, everything smelled burned—like one giant barbecue. Little burned twigs and ashes still drifted in the air.

Bud Preston hopped out of the cab. Minnie got out of the other door. "We got your note you left at the ranch, Riley," Bud said. "So we came to get you."

Bud looked at Judd and smiled. "Listen, young fella," he said. "We owe a lot to you. The firefighters told us your firebreak helped make a difference. And wetting down the roof. The irrigation kept embers from catching fire in the grass. The animals are safe too."

Judd felt a rush of pride. He looked down at his boots.

"It'll take a while to round all the animals up," Bud added. "But I reckon we'll have some help."

"We'll all help," Whit assured him.

"We're so glad everything is safe," Arella said.

Minnie smiled. "We are too," she said.

Riley stared at the ground. Did the fire make Riley finally realize how special the valley was? Judd wondered. Did it finally mean something to him?

"Come on, Riley," Bud said. "We have work to do."

Riley grabbed his backpack. "See ya, Judd," he said. He held a hand up in a sort of wave. He stopped. "Uh— and thanks. Thanks for everything," he added gruffly. Then he hopped in the cab.

Judd was surprised. Riley never thanked anyone for anything. Maybe something good would come out of this fire after all.

Judd stared out at the blackened hills. All those trees gone. What devastation, he thought. And they had almost lost their ranch.

Why were people so careless? Like those campers. Didn't they understand the trouble and danger a fire caused?

Smoke still rose in the air. But it was controlled now, thanks to Andy and all the firefighters.

Judd realized he was still a little shaky. But he felt proud. And someday, he could be saving ranches and forests too. If only he could convince his dad.

The Prestons' truck pulled out of the yard.

Whit looked at Judd. A smile tugged at the corners of his mouth. "Well, Judd," he said. "I guess you proved yourself today." His smile grew. "I have to admit, I'm proud of you. Teddy told us how you even went to rescue Riley too."

Judd blinked. What was his dad saying?

"I guess maybe you're cut out to be a firefighter after all," Whit said. He looked at Judd. "But while you're living here, I still expect help with the ranch."

Judd's heart soared. Yes! His dad actually said he could be a firefighter!

"Thanks, Dad," Judd said. He tried not to grin too broadly.

"Well, let's saddle up," Whit said. "We need to help the Prestons get their stock back."

****

The next three days flew by. Ranch chores and rounding up stock filled the hours.

Judd had ridden over to the station Wednesday morning to get the latest news. But Andy said that Fire Investigation hadn't finished yet.

"Not yet, hotshot hero," Andy had kidded him. "They're still sifting the grid for evidence. They'll find what started it. Don't worry. We'll let you know, Sherlock!"

Then Koreene and her sister Ellen had ridden over late Wednesday afternoon. She, Teddy, Riley, and Ellen had all gone swimming in the pond with Judd.

Thursday morning came. Judd was feeding the horses. While he dipped buckets of oats, he thought about the last three days.

Riley had been a lot easier to get along with. He had been a lot quieter since the fire. He hardly said anything obnoxious. Judd frowned. It seemed as if Riley was doing a lot of thinking. About time, he snorted.

Riley hadn't been riding the motorcycle either. Judd sure didn't miss that noisy thing.

Judd looked up to see a bright red county fire department Jeep drive down the road toward the Prestons'. Why was it going there?

It wasn't the Wells Valley station Jeep. Who would it be? Oh yeah! It must be Fire Investigation. Would they come here next? Would they ask him and Riley questions about those two campers?

He looked down the road again. Dust still hung in the air from the Jeep.

Then Judd glanced up at the ranch house. He was

waiting for his dad. They were going to clean out drainage ditches today. But his dad wasn't out yet. Maybe he had time to ride over to the Prestons' right now. He couldn't wait to talk to the team!

Quickly, he brought out Cab, saddled her, and ran up the porch steps.

"I'm going over to the Prestons' for a few minutes," he hollered through the screen door. Then he turned and raced down again. He'd ride away before anyone could think twice and stop him. Tracker wagged his tail and followed.

They reached the Prestons'. The fire department Jeep was in the yard. The investigators must be inside.

Judd's heart raced in excitement. Now he'd get to hear what was going on! "Ho, girl," he told Cab. He slid off and tied her to the tie rail.

Judd knocked at the screen door.

"Come in," someone called. It sounded like Minnie. Her voice sounded strained.

Judd walked in. The three investigators were standing in the middle of the room.

Bud was standing next to Minnie. He had his arm around her. Bud looked tired.

Minnie's mouth was pressed in a thin line. Were those tears in her eyes? What was going on?

Riley's face was white. He was sitting on the sofa. He stared at his hands.

"Come on in, Judd," Bud said. He looked at Judd. "You might as well hear this too.

"This is Judd Vandorf," Bud said to the team. "He's our neighbor. He helped save our ranch."

"Oh, yes," the woman said. "Andy Carr told us all about you, Judd." She smiled. "Good work the other day."

Judd forced a smile. "Thanks," he answered.

Something was wrong here. What was going on?

"Riley," Bud said, "I think you might as well tell your friend." He looked at Riley.

Riley looked up at Judd for a moment. Then he looked down again. He began talking in a low voice. Judd could hardly hear him.

"I did it," he said. "I started the fire. I didn't know I did. Honest." He looked up at Judd for a moment. "But it was my fault. All of it."

Judd froze. Riley? But what about the campers?

Riley drew a quivering breath. He looked at everyone. "I didn't mean to, though." He stopped. "It was an accident." He looked pleadingly at the investigators.

"Yes, it was accidental," one of the men said. "But it's still a misdemeanor. We'll have to take you in and book you."

Book Riley? Riley was being arrested? Judd couldn't believe his ears!

"Then we'll release you to the custody of your parents," the woman said. "There will be a big fine. You'll be on probation."

"We'll also have to talk about recovering the cost of putting out the fire," one of the men added.

Judd's head reeled in shock. He couldn't believe what he was hearing.

"His parents, eh?" Bud said. He paused. He looked at Minnie, raising his eyebrows. She nodded.

"Is it possible to get him released to our custody instead?" he asked. "We've been thinking about having him live with us this coming school year."

Bud looked at Riley. Riley stared at the carpet.

"We think he's making some good changes up here. His parents would like him to be up here too," Bud added. "They've asked us already."

"We'll have to settle this with the juvenile authorities," the woman said. "But as far as we're concerned, it's all right with us."

Riley looked up at his grandparents. His eyes were red.

"Tha-thanks," he mumbled. "I-I'd like to stay up here. You-you really want me?" he asked.

Judd felt embarrassed. Poor Riley. Imagine not feeling wanted anywhere.

"You bet, son," Bud said.

"Of course, Riley," Minnie said. She walked over to Riley and hugged him.

Judd looked at the woman investigator. "How did you find out it was Riley?" he asked. "I thought it was those two campers."

"We sifted the area. We found the point of origin. And we found two tiny pieces of carbon," she said.

The woman looked over at Riley. He was covering

his face with his hands.

"Carbon like that comes only from a motorcycle," the investigator added. "A motorcycle without a spark arrester." She frowned.

Bud shook his head. "We hounded you about that, Riley. You told us you put it on." He sighed. "If we're going to be a family, we need to be honest with each other from now on. All three of us," he said looking from Riley to Minnie.

"But we want you here. And we'll do everything we can to make it work," Minnie added.

"Riley *helped* with the fire too," Judd said quickly. "He helped clear brush and stuff. And we let the animals out."

"All of that will be taken into consideration," the woman said.

Everyone walked outside together. Riley got into the red Jeep with the investigators. Bud and Minnie got into their truck. Judd noticed that Riley looked pale.

"See you later," Riley said.

"Yeah," Judd said. He raised a hand.

Judd swung onto Cab. He watched as the two vehicles drove off.

"Well, let's go, Cab," he said. "Looks like we have our work cut out for us this year with Riley around."

Cab tossed her head. Judd grinned.

"Aw, maybe he's not such a bad guy after all," Judd said aloud. "A year in Wells Valley should fix him up just fine!" And he kicked Cab into a canter for home.